I Call It Sky

I Call It Sky

Will C. Howell
Illustrations by John Ward

Walker and Company

New York

Every morning,
when sunlight jumps through
my window,
I burst out the door.
I am surrounded by air.
It nips at my nose
and tosses my hair.
It is inside me when I breathe,
and it is outside me
everywhere.

In the summer,
the warm air is quiet.
It does not move much.

But sometimes
the warm air wakes up
and glides by my face
just enough to kiss my cheek.
I call it a breeze.

In the fall, the air
grows wet and heavy.
It huddles close to the ground.
I cannot see through it.
I call this fog.

Sometimes wet air gathers
in big black bunches of clouds.
When the clouds get too heavy,
they squeeze out rain.

In the winter,
clouds freeze
and shiver
and they toss down the snow
instead.

In the spring,
I feel the air dash and dart around me.
It rages through the trees
and sweeps the ground.
I call it wind.

I know all about air.
It is the place where birds soar.

It teases the grass . . .

and makes me warm or cold.

I know about the quiet summer air
because I can see the still flowers
resting on green picket stems.

I know about a summer breeze
because I can hear it
stirring the leaves
nesting in the branches.
I like to listen
to the secrets it whispers to me.

I know about fog in the fall
because I can step into it
and feel its wetness hide me.
I like to disappear into the fog
and pretend that I am
invisible.

I know about rain
because I can feel its drops
tickle my eyelashes
and trickle over the tip of my nose.
I like to stand under my umbrella
and watch the raindrops
splash at my feet.

I know about the snow
because I can stick out my tongue
and taste it.
I like to run after snowflakes,
which flutter down
like a million white butterflies,
and catch them.

I know about the wind
in the spring
because it carries the smells
of the new grass
and fresh flowers
and leads me into the fields
where they grow.
I like to run with my kite
and play tug-of-war
with the wind.

Every night,
when the stars begin to
pop into their places,
I am surrounded by air.
It slips under my clothes
and trails me into the house.
It fills up my room
and sits on the edge of my bed.

Even when I cannot see it
or catch it in my hands
or taste it
or smell it
or feel it on my face,
I still know the air is there.
It welcomes the sun in the morning
and frames the stars at night.
I call it sky.

To Meindert DeJong, for his excellence and encouragement. —W. C. H.

To Delesha, Uncle John. —J. W.

Text copyright © 1999 by Will C. Howell
Illustrations © 1999 by John Ward

First published in the United States of America in 1999 by Walker Publishing Company, Inc.

Published simultaneously in Canada by Fitzhenry and Whiteside, Markham, Ontario L3R 4T8

Library of Congress Cataloging-in-Publication Data
Howell, Will C.
I call it sky/Will C. Howell; illustrations by John Ward.
p.   cm.
Summary: Children enjoy the summer breeze, fall fog, winter snow, and spring wind.
ISBN 0-8027-8677-4 (hardcover). —ISBN 0-8027-8678-2 (reinforced)
[1. Weather—Fiction. 2. Seasons—Fiction.] I.Ward, John (John Clarence), ill. II. Title.
PZ7.H8387Iae   1999
[Fic]—dc21   98-49053
                                                                CIP
                                                                AC

Book design by Sophie Ye Chin

PRINTED IN HONG KONG

10 9 8 7 6 5 4 3 2 1

Afterword

I call it sky, but I am really talking about the atmosphere, the air that surrounds Earth. Our atmosphere reaches nearly one hundred miles out from Earth, but clouds and rain and wind all happen just in the first six to ten miles, called the *troposphere*.

Although I can walk through the atmosphere as if it were empty, it is not empty at all. The atmosphere is kept quite busy managing its temperature, moisture, air pressure, and wind.

The atmosphere absorbs the same sun that jumps through my window and keeps it from escaping too quickly back into space. This is called the greenhouse effect. The degree of heat in the atmosphere is called temperature.

Just as the sun warms me, it also warms the water that is in lakes and streams and puddles. The warm water turns to vapor, like steam from a teakettle, and goes up into the atmosphere. This is called evaporation. Sometimes the warm moisture in the air begins to cool on its way up and forms a mist. When the air cools near the ground, it forms low clouds we call fog.

As air goes higher it expands and cools. Cool air cannot hold as much water vapor as warm air can. The water vapor condenses and changes to tiny droplets of water. Billions of these tiny droplets form clouds. When these droplets get so heavy that the air can no longer hold them, they fall back to Earth as rain. If the temperature is below freezing, ice crystals form and fall down to Earth as snow.

Just as the sun's heat causes water to turn into vapor and mix with the air, it also causes the air to flow around Earth. Gravity pulls the atmosphere toward Earth. The force of the atmosphere pushing down on Earth is called air pressure.

Cool air weighs more than warm air and puts more pressure on Earth than does warm air. The movement of the air from high pressure areas (cool air) to low pressure areas (warm air) is what makes wind.

So much is happening in this thing that I call sky. It is all around me, and it is inside me. When I breathe in the air, my lungs keep the oxygen that my body needs. Then I breathe the rest back out into the air around me. In a way, I am a part of the atmosphere, and it is a part of me.